98° backstage pass

Meet 98° [left to right] Nick Lachey, Drew Lachey, Jeff Timmons, Justin Jeffre

SCHOLASTIC INC.

New York   Toronto   London   Auckland   Sydney
Mexico City   New Delhi   Hong Kong

Front Cover: Anthony Cutajar;   Back Cover: Anthony Cutajar/London Features;   1: Anthony Cutajar
3: Michael Benabib;   4: Anthony Cutajar/London Features;   5: Janet Macoska;   6, top: Janet Macoska;   6, bottom: Janet Macoska;   7, top: Janet Macoska;   7, bottom: Janet Macoska;   8: Bob Mussell/Retna;   9: Fitzroy Barrett/Globe Photos;   10: Anthony Cutajar/London Features;   11, top: Eddie Malluk;   11, bottom: Bob Mussell/Retna;   12: Anthony Cutajar;   13, left: Walter McBride/Retna;   13, right: Anthony Cutajar;   14: Anthony Cutajar;   15, both: Eddie Malluk;   16, top: Eddie Malluk;   16, bottom: Anthony Cutajar;   17: Anthony Cutajar/London Features;   18: Anthony Cutajar/London Features;   19, top: Janet Macoska;   19, bottom: Bob Mussell/Retna;   20, top: Eddie Malluk;   20, bottom: Janet Macoska;   21, top: Anthony Cutajar;   21, bottom: Janet Macoska;   22: London Features;   23: Anthony Cutajar/London Features;   24-25: Michael Benabib;   26: Anthony Cutajar/London Features;   27, top: Janet Macoska;   27, middle: Eddie Malluk;   27, bottom: Janet Macoska;   28, top: Anthony Cutajar;   28, bottom: Ernie Paniccioli;   29, top: Anthony Cutajar;   29, bottom: Walter McBride/Retna;   30, top: John Ricard/Retna;   30, bottom: Walter McBride/Retna;   31: Walter McBride/Retna;   32, top: Eddie Malluk;   32, bottom: Ernie Paniccioli;   33, both: Joey Delvalle/courtesy NBC, Inc.;   34: Ann Bogart;   35, top: Janette Beckman/Retna;   35, bottom: Ernie Paniccioli;   36: Walter McBride/Retna   37: Eddie Malluk;   38, top: Ernie Paniccioli;   38, bottom: Eddie Malluk;   39: Ann Bogart;   40, top, both and bottom left: Fitzroy Barrett/Globe;   40, bottom right: N. Zuffante/Star File Photo;   41, top: Gregg DeGuire/London Features;   41, bottom: Steve Granitz/Retna;   42, top left: Eddie Malluk;   42, top right: Anthony Cutajar   42, bottom left: Walter McBride/Retna;   42, bottom right: Eddie Malluk;   45: Michael Benabib   46: Anthony Cutajar/London Features;   47, top: Janet Macoska;   47, bottom left: Walter McBride/Retna   47, bottom right: Anthony Cutajar;   48: Anthony Cutajar/London Features

ISBN 0-439-08710-4

12 11 10 9 8 7 6 5 4 3 2   9/9 0 1 2 3 4/0

Printed in the U.S.A.
First Scholastic printing, April 1999

Enter the World of 98°

A couple of years ago, the names Nick Lachey, Drew Lachey, Jeff Timmons, and Justin Jeffre were foreign to music fans around the world. But ever since the release of their self-titled debut album, *98°*, in July 1997, this four-some from Ohio has gone from "Invisible Men" (the name of their first single, of course, was "Invisible Man") to superstars! How'd it happen?

This amazing scrapbook gives you the inside scoop, plus tons of color photos on these four hum-ble guys who had a big dream and a whole lot of talent. Here's the real relationship between adorable brothers Nick and Drew, plus individual chapters on each guy, their love-o-scopes, and little-known facts you absolutely have to know! You'll be a 98° expert with this awesome Backstage Pass!

Can't fight the fever — 98° is comin' atcha!

Contents

Chapter One
Getting Together

When Nick and Drew Lachey were growing up in Cincinnati, Ohio, they always knew they could sing. Their parents encouraged their vocal talents, and the guys took singing seriously enough to enroll in Cincinnati's School for the Creative and Performing Arts, a high school for budding actors, artists, dancers, and vocalists. That's where Nick met Justin Jeffre, who was also an aspiring singer. Meanwhile, Jeff Timmons, who lived in Massillon, Ohio (across the state from the other three guys), was a sports fanatic with plans to become a pro football player. He had absolutely no idea he'd end up singing to sold-out crowds all over the world!

In fact, if you go back just a few years, none of them could have predicted they'd even be together in a singing group, let alone one as successful as 98°. Their story is a circuitous one — pay attention, there'll be a quiz later!

Nick and Justin: Best Buds

During high school, Nick and Justin became the best of friends. They sang in choir together and even performed in a barbershop quartet at a nearby amusement park called King's Island. After graduation, Justin and Nick joined an oldies band called the Avenues, in which they played horns as well as sang. But success — in terms of making a living at it — eluded them.

Eventually, they both opted for college and "fallback" careers. Nick attended the University of Southern California and then transferred to Miami University of Ohio, where he majored in sports medicine. Justin enrolled in the University of Cincinnati and went for a degree in history.

Drew's Path

Drew, two and a half years younger than his big bro, loved music, too. But not exclusively — he had other aspirations. When high school was over, he joined the army. His dream was to end up working for a search and rescue team in Colorado. So, after his stint in the military, he moved to New York and utilized his army medic training, working as an EMT (emergency medical technician).

Drew Lachey

SOUND BYTE: "We were sitting at home in L.A. in our two-bedroom apartment and we were trying to come up with a name for the group and we wanted a name that would create a mood. So, we thought, What's hot? 98° is what we came up with." — Drew

Jeff's Journey

The guy least likely to become a singer was definitely Jeff Timmons. Convinced that he had a shot at a career in sports, Jeff entered Kent State University with gridiron fantasies. His academic major was psychology, but he played football every chance he could. And then, he changed directions entirely.

One day, while kidding around with some college friends, Jeff sang for a few girls. They immediately complimented him on his amazing tenor voice and gave him an idea: Why not make singing a career?

Intrigued with the idea, Jeff moved out to Los Angeles. He put together a singing group that included his older brother Mike. They called themselves Just Us. Though they sounded great, two of the guys quit the band to pursue other projects. While trying to get another group going, Jeff decided to try his luck at acting. He scored a commercial for the U.S. Navy.

Jeff Timmons

During the audition rounds, Jeff met John Lippmann, another young singer/actor wannabe. John was a fellow Ohioan, who'd attended Cincinnati's School for the Creative and Performing Arts. At first, that meant nothing to Jeff, but it soon would. Along with Jeff's brother, Mike, a new group was forming. It would take one more person to complete it.

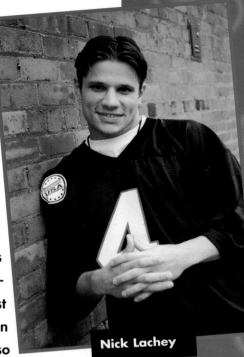

Nick Lachey

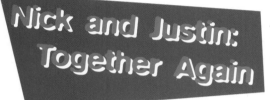

Nick and Justin: Together Again

That's where Nick came in. John knew Nick from high school and thought Nick's tenor voice would blend perfectly. In 1995, Nick jumped at the opportunity to return to his first love, singing. He flew to Los Angeles almost immediately! When Jeff's brother Mike quit, Nick called his old buddy Justin, who also loved the idea of giving music a second shot.

Still using the name Just Us, they were far from an overnight success. The foursome made ends meet by working as security guards, busboys, delivery boys, and other odd jobs. Appearances at talent shows and practice, practice, practice were how they honed their four-part harmony sound. They even snagged a gig singing the national anthem at an L.A. Dodgers baseball game.

The Big Break

Justin Jeffre

Their major break arrived the day Boyz II Men came to town. In the naive hope that they'd get to sing for the Boyz, they snuck backstage and crooned "In the Still of the Night." It didn't work — exactly. The Boyz never got to hear them, but a talent scout from an L.A. radio station did, and asked them to sing on the air. That, in turn, brought them to the attention of music manager Paris D'Jon, who promptly signed them up.

SOUND BYTE: "Boy bands are more dancers and performers than singers. We pride ourselves on always singing live. It's singing first." — Nick, to *Popstar!*

Drew, Take Two

Drew, meanwhile, was working in New York. He loved his job, but had never quite gotten over the desire to sing. So when, out of the blue, John up and quit the group, Drew jumped at the chance to join his brother. He recalls that fateful call from Nick like it was yesterday. "I quit my job, closed my bank account, packed up my car, and picked Nick up at Newark Airport," Drew told *Tiger Beat* magazine. "I made the three-day trek out to L.A. where I learned the group's music. Two days after I got there, we opened for Montell [Jordan] at the House of Blues."

Record Deal

Before long, tons of record companies were buzzing about this slammin' quartet, now christened 98°. On April 3, 1996, Nick, Drew, Justin, and Jeff signed with Motown Records, home to such musical legends as Boyz II Men, Stevie Wonder, and Marvin Gaye. And now, home to 98° too.

RANDOM FACT: Before they decided to go with 98°, they considered names like Forte, Inertia, and Next Issue.

Dressing alike is a sometime thing: they jumped into red at Nickelodeon's *The Big Help*.

Drew

Chapter Two
Drew's Deal

E ven though he's the youngest member of 98°, 22-year-old Drew is definitely the dude who keeps things together. He's extremely sensible and organized — if the guys have to catch a plane or get to a talk show, you can be sure Drew's the one to get everyone in gear. As a matter of fact, when ambitious Drew was little, he was the first Lachey brother to attend Cincinnati's School for the Creative and Performing Arts. He got Nick to audition the following year.

Another side of Drew is his natural instinct to help people. That's why a career as an emergency medical technician wasn't a bad choice for him. But his incredible love for singing (and big bro Nick) eventually brought him back to performing. And he wouldn't have it any other way. "I love the adrenaline rush of being on stage, being there, totally open, having everybody watch you and the rush of that," he said in an interview with *Teen Machine* magazine. With his hazel eyes and melt-your-heart smile, it's no surprise that Drew has attracted lots of loyal fans.

In concert, Drew pours it on. Why? "Because of you."

Drew trades off lead vocals with his brother Nick and bandmates Jeff and Justin.

When he's on the road with 98°, Drew's the band's unofficial photographer. "I've had so many experiences, it'd be impossible to remember them all. So I take a lot of pictures," he told *Popstar!* magazine. Traveling around the world, from Asia to Europe, Canada, and beyond, Drew's amassed quite a collection of snaps. But, in spite of all the fame and acclaim, Drew's still the same down-to-earth guy he's always been.

Vital Stats

Full name: Andrew John Lachey
Nicknames: Drew, Sprout
Birth date: August 8, 1976
Birthplace: Cincinnati, Ohio
Zodiac sign: Leo
Height: 5'6"
Hair: Brown
Eyes: Hazel
Parents: Cate Fopma-Leimbach and John Lachey
Sibs: Older bro Nick, younger bros Isaac and Zach; younger sister Josie
Vocal part: Baritone

Sometimes Drew poses without his trademark backward baseball cap — but not often!

Faves

Music: "I've got eclectic tastes, classic rock and R&B, but also jazz and classical," he told *Teen* magazine, citing Lauryn Hill, Led Zeppelin, and Lenny Kravitz as examples.
Song: "Purple Rain" by Prince
Foods: Pizza, donuts, any and all junk food
Color: Navy blue
Sports: Waterskiing and snowboarding
Clothing line: Tommy Hilfiger
Movie: *Braveheart*
Vacation place: "A little cabin in the mountains or anywhere far from cars and noise."

Drew Quotes

On his name: "Never, never call me Andy — it's a complete no-no. No one's ever called me that and no one ever will."

On his baseball hat fetish: "Well, if someday I feel like doing my hair, you might see me without a baseball hat. But for the most part, I'm just too lazy."

On being a role model: "It's kind of fun. We feel like we're pretty clean-cut, good guys who don't do anything bad so it's not a big pressure. We just feel kind of privileged that people are looking at us for a little bit of guidance and kind of as an example."

Fast Facts

Pet peeve: Rude people. That's a Drew no-no!
Special memory: When his little brother Isaac was born
How he chills out: He listens to music or works out.

Drew's nickname is "the baby," since he's the youngest group member.

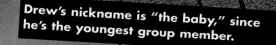

Drew at an autograph session — meeting fans is very cool.

Nick

Chapter Three
Nick's News

Nick's heart beats true — especially when he sings for you.

Clutching a fan-tossed bouquet, Nick takes an H_2O break.

O ften called the voice of 98°, Nick is the stellar singer whose clear, dulcet tones can be heard crooning on hits like "Invisible Man" and "Because of You." Yet the 25-year-old doesn't consider himself the lead singer of the group — he's the first to boast about the *other* guys.

Being a team player is nothing new to Nick, whose plans to become a sports hero ended pretty early on. "My childhood goal was to be a football player. Then I went to a performing arts school with no sports," he told *Popstar!*

Nick is 98°'s official worrywart. He frets about everything — from their harmonies, to the song lineup in concert, to their stage outfits, to their chart position. Yet his concern for all things 98° isn't such a bad thing — he just needs to chill a little bit. For Nick knows that all the stressing over business stuff can't be good for his creativity or his music. And that's totally where his heart beats.

In fact, Nick's tickled about everything having to do with being part of 98°, especially the cool stuff he gets to experience every day, even if some of it is way weird and wacky, like the time he got his hair dyed blue for an E!-TV segment. But the best is this: "Getting to meet people you'd never get to meet, see places you'd never get to see, do things you'd never get to do. It's everything I imagined as a kid, when I dreamed of being a rock star."

Vital Stats

Full name: Nicholas Scott Lachey
Nicknames: Hollywood, Slider
Birth date: November 9, 1973
Birthplace: Harlan, Kentucky
Zodiac sign: Scorpio
Height: 5'10"
Hair: Brown is Nick's natural color, but he often sports blond highlights.
Eyes: Blue
Parents: Cate Fopma-Leimbach and John Lachey
Sibs: Younger bros Drew, Isaac, and Zach; younger sister Josie
Vocal part: Second tenor

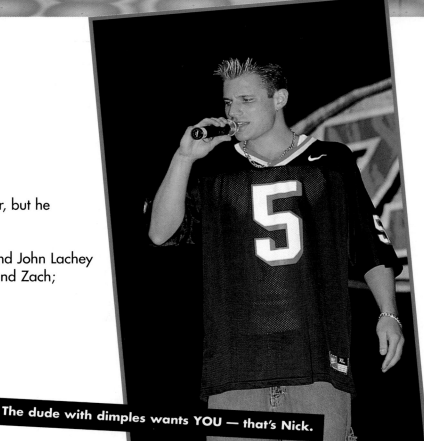

The dude with dimples wants YOU — that's Nick.

Faves

Music: "I like everything from classic rock to heavy metal to rap to R&B. I've been listening to OutKast and Rush lately," he mentioned in *Teen*.
Song: "Cherish the Day" by Sade
Foods: Skyline chili, steak, pizza, and barbecue
Color: Red
Sports: Football and basketball
Clothing line: Phat Farm
Movie: *Die Hard*
Vacation places: Hawaii and Florida

Nick flicks the sign of the L — for love?!

Random Fact

Nick found out the hard way that traveling on the road means packing light! "At first I was an idiot. I had two suitcases and I'm like, 'What am I carrying all this around for in the middle of summer?' I quickly learned not to do that."

Things That Make Nick Tick

• Watching ESPN! He's crazy for hometown teams like football's Cincinnati Bengals and baseball's Cincinnati Reds.

• Listening to his stereo, his most prized possession.

• Meeting other celebrities. Nick counts the band 'N Sync and actress Jennifer Love Hewitt as good friends.

Jeff

Chapter Four
Just Jeff

Jeff is the most ready-to-smile member of 98° and he's got the kind of megawatt grin that lights up a room. He's also a really modest guy. And that's exactly the way he's always been. When you ask the other members about Jeff, they'll immediately say that he's the one to cheer everyone up when they're down.

It wasn't until Jeff turned 20 years old that singing — let alone professionally — was even on the radar screen. Like Nick, Jeff always longed to jump into professional sports. Or, if that didn't pan out, he toyed with the idea of becoming a pediatrician or a child psychologist. Music was never on the agenda. Though he did some performing with his high school choir, Jeff would've laughed if you told him back then that he was destined to make singing a career. "Most of the training I got vocally has been through this group," he told *Tiger Beat*. So it was kind of amazing that once he discovered his talent and love for music, he had the guts to follow his heart and try his hand at the notoriously competitive profession. It was a decision he wouldn't regret.

Besides his sweet tenor voice, this 25-year-old super cutie is known for his amazingly fit body. But he has to train very hard for his six-pack abs and sculpted muscles. "I work out a couple of times a week. When I go, I just do heavy weights and low reps. Lots of stretching too, which keeps you toned and conditioned." In homage to the group, Jeff (like Nick and Drew) has a 98° tattoo on his right arm. It's a constant reminder of how much the group he founded means in his life. That's Jeff for you — he doesn't take anything for granted.

Jeff's nickname is "the hot one," and it's easy to see why.

In concert, Jeff gets with the ballads, soulfully.

Vital Stats

Full name: Jeffrey Brandon Timmons
Nickname: Sugar
Birth date: April 30, 1973
Birthplace: Canton, Ohio
Zodiac sign: Taurus
Height: 5'8"
Hair: Brown
Eyes: Blue
Parents: Patricia and James Timmons
Sibs: Older bro Mike; younger sister Tina
Vocal part: First tenor

How proud is Jeff to be a Degree? The proof's in the tattoo!

Just Jeff — the boy who went from college cutie to serious singer in no time!

Faves

Singers: Brian McKnight, Shania Twain
Song: "It's So Hard to Say Goodbye to Yesterday" by Boyz II Men
Foods: Seafood and steak
Colors: Orange and blue
Sport: Football
Clothing line: Phat Farm
Movie: *The Shawshank Redemption*
Vacation place: Panama City, Florida

Jeff takes a photo op break and does that half-smile thing for the camera.

RANDOM FACT: Of all the guys in the group, Jeff's the most likely to become a major producer one day. Though he loves performing, Jeff really enjoys the technical side of being in the studio and working out 98°'s famous harmonies.

Candid Quote:

"We're all very grounded guys, we all have a spiritual background. We have the proper perspective. We know as easily as [fame] comes, it can easily be taken away. You should enjoy it while you have it."

Funny Moments

• The time he was singing on stage and his overalls clip came off. "They just fell down. I went redder than you can imagine."
• When he mistook starch for hairspray. His hair didn't smell so good, but it certainly stayed in place.

Taking time to meet the fans is primo: Jeff takes a pic with 12-year-old Clevelander Ryan Kaston.

They admit it: singing love songs suits them best.

Q & A Craziness

The best way to hear the scoop on 98° is straight from the guys!

Have you guys always been so close?

JUSTIN: I think it was pretty odd how we naturally fit. We seemed to get along really well from the beginning. We lived in a two-bedroom apartment, had hard times and no money. But we got along amazingly well.

With whom would you most like to collaborate musically?

NICK: Brian [McKnight] because he is so very gifted and talented and a very cool guy. A collaboration with a group like Bush would be great because we, as a group, are always looking to do something different.

Drew, how would you describe your other 98°'s bandmates?

DREW: Justin drags us all out and makes us see the cities we're in. He's just real chill, and he's the comic relief with all his one-liners. Nick is the, I-don't-wanna-say, spokesman. He's the natural loudmouth. Even if you don't agree with what he's saying, he makes sure you think about it. Jeff gets such an enjoyment out of it all. He makes it very known that he loves what he's doing. Me, I'm just a bum along for the ride (laughs).

What's the best advice you could give young aspiring musicians?

JEFF: Have faith in everything you do. And have faith that the outcome is going to be like you want it to be and it will, definitely.

What's the best thing about being in 98°?

NICK: For us, it's all about the fans and the music. We try to involve the audience and make them feel like a part of the show.

Justin, you seem to be the mellowest guy in the band. How do you stay so laid-back?

JUSTIN: I think that I'm a pretty laid-back guy just in general. I think that there's times when you need to worry about things and then there's times when you can't control them anyway. I personally believe that things happen for a reason. If you work hard, even if you don't get exactly where you thought you'd get to, you'll see that the result is a good thing.

Where would you like to see the band in five years?

JEFF: Just doing what we're doing right now. As long as we can do music and sing and have fun and enjoy doing it and affect people in a positive way, I think that we'll be doing this for a long time. It's all about having fun and enjoying ourselves and as long as people accept us as a group, we're gonna still be singing.

Your fans are amazingly supportive. They seem to know everything about 98°.

DREW: Girls in Canada have pen pals in Asia and they send each other e-mail stuff and tell them to look out for us. It's like our fans are networking on the computer, setting stuff up for us. It's really amazing—they know more about us than we do!

"It's all about the fans and it's all about the music." — 98°

Justin

Chapter Five
Chilling With Justin

Cool, laid-back, and mellow are three perfect ways to describe Justin, the bass man of 98°. "I am very calm and natural," he's described himself. "I think things over a lot before making a decision, I think of the positives and negatives." When it came to deciding whether or not to join 98°, there was only one possible answer — a resounding yesss! Justin's deep, resonant voice is the perfect counterpoint to the baritone and tenor stylings of Drew, Nick, and Jeff. That's what makes them blend so well.

Growing up, Justin was bashful, a trait he's finally over. As a history major in college, Justin would sit in the back of class and barely say a word. That all changed when he joined 98°. Today, Justin speaks up for what he wants, and is having the time of his life! "I used to be one of the shyest people you would ever meet, but as I got older I found that it's important to live life to the fullest and don't be afraid to make a fool of yourself and have fun," he told *16* magazine.

Within the group, Justin is the funky, kooky one who's bleached his hair platinum blond and wears sunglasses 24–7. It's rare to see him without his shades, especially because fans keep sending him pairs all the time. "It's great and very cheap — well, cheap for me anyway," he quips. Despite his wild and crazy appearance, deep down Justin is a really sensitive guy who wants to make the most of his fame. He's determined to find new ways for 98° to give back to the community.

Justin belts out a power ballad — he's one of the groups main songwriters, too.

A reach out and touch moment onstage for Justin at a radio station event.

At an autograph session in Cleveland, Justin shakes hands with a lucky fan — the group is also known for giving hugs.

Vital Stats

Full name: Justin Paul Jeffre
Nicknames: Droopy, Big J
Birth date: February 25, 1973
Birthplace: Mount Clemens, Michigan
Zodiac sign: Pisces
Height: 5'10"
Hair: Brown
Eyes: Blue
Parents: Sue and Dan Jeffre
Sibs: Older bro Dan; younger sister Alexandra
Vocal part: Bass

Faves

Singers: Brian McKnight, Bob Marley, James Brown, and Stevie Wonder
Song: "Try a Little Tenderness" by Otis Redding
Foods: Pizza, donuts, and Skyline chili
Color: Blue
Sports: Soccer and tennis
Clothing line: Ralph Lauren, Phat Farm, and DKNY
Movie: *Braveheart*
Vacation places: Los Angeles, and Santa Fe, New Mexico

Judging by their jerseys, Drew is not a huge fan of basketball, but Nick roots for the Los Angeles Clippers, Jeff's an Orlando Magic fan, while Justin's an L.A. Lakers kinda guy.

He may be dressed for the Arctic Circle, but wherever Justin Jeffre goes, it's always . . . 98°!

"Justin's the mack daddy, he's like the too-cool member of the group."
— Nick on Justin

Random Facts

• Justin was shocked when he learned he had such a low-register voice after returning from summer break one year. "I was in choir at school singing soprano and alto, and when I came back [after] one summer, they put me in the bass section."

• People who smoke really gross Justin out. The smell of it makes him sick!

Justin Up Close

On making a difference: "[My goal] is to be big enough where we can really have an impact on certain things. I always want to make a difference."

On meeting his idol Stevie Wonder: "I'd have to say that's honestly the highlight of my career so far."

Felt-tipped Sharpie pen at the ready, Justin does the autograph session thing at New York City's Motown Cafe.

The Real Deal on 98°

When a group gets as big as 98°, there are bound to be rumors. Here's the truth—and nothing but—about Drew, Nick, Jeff, and Justin!

RUMOR: Nick is engaged to be married.

TRUTH: Not! All of the guys are seriously single.

RUMOR: 98°'s fans are so crazy for them, they've even hidden in laundry carts at the guys' hotels when they're on tour.

TRUTH: Yup. 98°'s admirers will go to major lengths to get close to these cuties. One fan even flew from the Czech Republic to New York just to attend one of their in-store appearances! Now that's dedication.

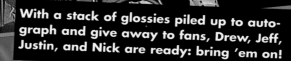

With a stack of glossies piled up to autograph and give away to fans, Drew, Jeff, Justin, and Nick are ready: bring 'em on!

RUMOR: Nick and Drew's mom pushed them into show business.

TRUTH: Far from it. Their mom Cate was actually pretty worried about her two boys becoming singers. "My mom was a little skeptical at the beginning," Nick says. "But even when she didn't agree 100% with what we were doing, she still backed us up." Today, she runs 98°'s fan club!

RUMOR: Drew likes classical music.

TRUTH: Very true. His favorite classical piece is by American composer Samuel Barber, called "Adagio for Strings."

RUMOR: Jeff dated Mariah Carey.

TRUTH: Of course Jeff thinks she's pretty, but he's never dated the diva. Actually, the rumor got started when Jeff was spotted with his bud, singer Samantha Cole, who could pass for Mariah's sis.

RUMOR: 98° got bumped up to first class on a flight to Hawaii when they asked if they could sing in exchange for the switch!

TRUTH: Absolutely. Hey, when you've got talent like these guys, why not use it? Also, on that same trip to Hawaii, they were spotted by some fans and got to go jet skiing for free. Not too bad.

RUMOR: In their starving artist days, the guys once slept on mattresses they found in the garbage!

TRUTH: Jeff admits, "We did sleep on mattresses that we pulled out of the garbage." But, of course, they cleaned them first!

Hometown boys make good — 98° is back home in Ohio.

Whoo-hoo! The album, *98° and Rising* goes gold — and the single, "Because of You," hits the platinum peak.

Is Drew a New York Yankee fan? Let's just say that he's a baseball cap fan!

RUMOR: All the guys in 98° want to get matching pierced eyebrows.
TRUTH: Nope. They've got pierced ears and that's absolutely enough for them!

RUMOR: 98° are jealous of the success of other boy groups like 'N Sync and Backstreet Boys.
TRUTH: Double nope! "We think that groups such as 'N Sync and Backstreet are talented and deserve their success," Justin says.

98° Does City Guys!

RUMOR: Nick serenades Cassidy (played by Marissa Dyan) on the "Dance Fever" episode of NBC's Saturday morning sitcom, *City Guys* (originally aired in October 1998).

TRUTH: The proof is in the video. In June 1998, the guys flew to NBC's soundstage in Burbank, California, for two days of rehearsing and taping. In the episode, Cassidy is dating 98°'s Nick, but nobody believes her. She asks Nick if he and the rest of the group would come and perform at a rooftop party to prove to her friends she's telling the truth. Nick promises they'll try, even though the guys are in the midst of recording at the studio. He makes it—of course—and the moment is a romantic dream come true!

What was it like for the guys to perform on the TV show *City Guys*?

The cast and crew made them feel totally comfortable, though Nick admits being a little nervous about playing himself on camera. (He was the only Degree with an actual speaking line.) Nick noted, "I was asking myself, "You're playing yourself—how hard can that really be?"

But it is a different scenario. And it is different than being in front of the cameras for a video or something. The rest of the guys just had to keep their minds on remembering the lyrics of "I Do (Cherish You)" from their hit album *98° and Rising*. Rehearsing for the show was just as intense as a sound-check for a concert, but the quartet likes to get things right, so they appreciated the practice. Plus, Nick and the guys have done so many television appearances, they didn't mind wearing the heavy makeup for the cameras. It's just one of the hazards of showbiz!

In the beginning, there was Ohio — that was home. But California beckoned, and the young band went west, where they did a guest stint on the NBC show *City Guys*.

Chapter Six
Rising to the Top

Once they got signed to Motown Records, life became a whirlwind of activity for Drew, Jeff, Nick, and Justin. Since the release of that first album, *98°*, in 1997, the way-cute quartet has been in demand, big time. They sat for dozens of magazine and newspaper interviews, posed for a plethora of photo shoots, and made TV appearances on such high-profile shows as *Ricki Lake*, *CNN/Showbiz Today*, *E!-TV*, and *NBC Weekend Today*. And that was before their first single, "Invisible Man," went gold, selling over 500,000 copies. Next, they scored plenty of raves with "Was It Something I Didn't Say," the second song off their self-titled debut.

In addition to earning a reputation as sensitive balladeers, the guys got their share of the limelight as they toured across the country in their tailor-made Winnebago (which had their picture plastered on it!), as part of the *Seventeen* Magazine Live Tour. It introduced them to the world of fan mania, especially when they made guest appearances at cheerleading camps.

Jeff and Nick take a moment outside the studio.

Only two are biological bros, but 98° is all about brotherly love.

A Travelin' Band

98° also became world travelers, as they performed in concert all over the globe, from Canada to Asia, Germany, Indonesia, Malaysia, Singapore, Thailand, Hong Kong, Holland, and England. Unsurprisingly, fans in all corners of the world got turned onto them. "I was really surprised when we got off the plane in the Philippines, how acquainted the audience and our fans were with us," Nick has said. The sight of an entire concert hall singing every word to "Invisible Man" had a definite impact on these humble hotties!

Onstage, they are awesome. Unlike a lot of boy bands, 98° has never relied on flashy antics to take them through a show. Singing has always been the main entrée on a 98° menu — everything from up-tempo tunes to a cappella ballads. Harmony, sweet harmony, is what they're about. Being on the road nonstop not only made them better performers, their voices got even stronger.

The rare hatless, shot of Drew!

A Soundtrack Summer

Last summer was a big deal for 98° — they were invited to perform "True to Your Heart," the optimistic theme song to the Disney animated film *Mulan*. As if that weren't exciting enough — since it exposed them to an even bigger audience — the performance was a duet with the legendary Stevie Wonder, one of the guys' major idols. "True to Your Heart" even got them a coveted gig on TV's *The Tonight Show*, their most high-profile gig thus far. They were understandably nervous when they realized that millions of people would be tuning in, but, as always, the guys were absolutely amazing.

The Temperature's Rising

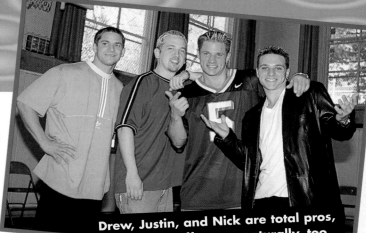

Drew, Justin, and Nick are total pros, but goofing off comes naturally, too.

Building on their accomplishments, 98° had big plans in store for their next album, *98° and Rising*, which was released on October 27, 1998. Mainly, the guys were ready to hit the music world by storm with their new collection of songs, many of which they wrote and produced themselves.

The hard work and anticipation was rewarded, big time. With hip-hop-influenced R&B (courtesy of Fugees star Pras, who produced the track "Fly With Me"), loads of ballads, and cool dance music, *98° and Rising* instantly became the album everyone was talking about. And listening to — and buying. Their first single, "Because of You" soared to platinum status (thanks especially to their breathtaking video atop San Francisco's Golden Gate Bridge) and the album itself went gold just five weeks after being on the charts.

Here, There, and Everywhere

The last few months of 1998 were a frenzy of activity for 98°: Everywhere you looked, there they were! They rode in the Macy's Thanksgiving Day Parade, and the Hollywood Christmas Day Parade, appeared on Nickelodeon's *The Big Help*, and on talk shows like *The View*.

In December, they kicked off their first major tour of North America, which Drew chatted to MTV about: "It's our first time in an actual, real-live tour bus. I mean, we've had our motor home — as a lot of people know — 'cause it's all over the country and stuff. But [this tour] is our first time with a real tour bus-type thing, with a PlayStation and a TV, and an actual driver. We don't have to drive ourselves."

A week before Christmas they performed at the super-popular Z-100 Jingle Ball concert in New York City alongside 'N Sync and Five. And they even got to spend New Year's Eve with bud Jennifer Love Hewitt as they helped host MTV's New Year's Eve Live show!

98° in '99

This year looks to be just as busy for the band. In January, they appeared on the American Music Awards, doing a tribute to Billy Joel. In February, 98° released their radio-only second single, "The Hardest Thing," and set off for a European tour with R&B superstars Dru Hill. They made stops in Switzerland, Germany, and England.

Spring brings 98° home, to headline the Heat It Up tour across Canada and the United States. They'll be hitting cities everywhere, so if they haven't already cut through your city or town, they might still be coming.

Their Greatest Joy: Giving Back

They take the cake: a home-baked gift from a talented fan.

But with all they've achieved, the accomplishment that gives them the most joy is the 98° Foundation, a charitable organization they established.

Nick explained a little about it at a press conference for Nickelodeon's *The Big Help*. "When we first started the group, we set up a foundation and over the last couple of years, we've had the pleasure of being affiliated with different charities — the New Edition Campaign [and] a charity called Habitat for Humanity, which builds houses for people who are less fortunate. We had the opportunity to go out on site and help build houses with them."

Gettin' huggy with Jennifer Love Hewitt is a definite perk.

Other charities they've given their time to are the Boys and Girls Clubs of America, Ronald McDonald House, the Inner City Games, and the NYU Children's Hospital. They've got plans to work with the Partnership for Drug-Free America, a cause all four of the guys are really passionate about.

Candid Quote:

"We went to the MTV Europe Awards in Rotterdam and we actually sat in the artist section. Steven Tyler and Aerosmith were right in front of us — U2 was right over there. BLACKstreet, Prodigy, Hanson, and Backstreet Boys were over there." — Nick

On-The-Road Bonding

"I think we understand how much we need each other for support and encouragement. Because being on the road you get so tired and beaten down by fatigue and stress that we need each other to pick ourselves back up and enjoy it again." — Drew

Feeling the Rhythm

"We're mainly just singing and kind of vibing with the music," Justin has said of their performing style. "But we're gonna start working on our new show soon and step up on every single aspect and do some more dancing."

Scary Moments

On filming the video for "Because of You": "To get up [to the top of the Golden Gate Bridge], it was like this real old and spooky elevator that only three people could squeeze into. It took six minutes going up, and the whole time you hear all these echoes. Then you get to the top and there's this porthole, like you're on a sub. You can see the whole bay and the wind is really whippin'. We were freakin' at first, but it wasn't dangerous, it was just . . . intense." — Nick

The Heat It Up Tour, So Far...

March 30, 1999	Seattle, WA	April 16, 1999	Pittsburgh, PA
March 31, 1999	Portland, OR	April 17, 1999	New York, NY
April 2, 1999	San Francisco, CA	April 18, 1999	Hartford, CT
April 3, 1999	Los Angeles, CA	April 20, 1999	Cleveland, OH
April 4, 1999	San Diego, CA	April 21, 1999	Harrisburg, PA
April 5, 1999	Las Vegas, NV	April 22, 1999	Philadelphia, PA
April 6, 1999	Salt Lake City, UT	April 23, 1999	Baltimore, MD
April 9, 1999	St. Louis, MO	April 24, 1999	Washington DC
April 10, 1999	Chicago, IL	April 25, 1999	Roanoke, VA
April 11, 1999	Detroit, MI	April 27, 1999	Norfolk, VA
April 13, 1999	Green Bay, WI	April 29, 1999	Charlotte, NC
April 14, 1999	Grand Rapids, MI	April 30, 1999	Charleston, SC
April 15, 1999	Buffalo, NY	May 1, 1999	Atlanta, GA

More to Come!

Check Your Local Newspaper!

Who knew they'd get so far, so fast? 98° worked hard —
but still they feel lucky.

Justin

Nick

The band was psyched about an appearance on Nickelodeon's *The Big Help* — volunteering in the community is something they totally believe in.

Jeff

Drew

98° was honored to be asked to sing on the *Mulan* soundtrack.

The guys heated up the stage during the American Music Awards tribute to Billy Joel in January 1999 with their HOT live performance of "Uptown Girl."

The brothers Lachey—Nick and Drew.

Drew's tattoo is almost identical to . . .
. . . the one on brother Nick's bicep
(see pic, top left).

Chapter Seven
Brotherly Love

Working and playing beside your brother is a whole lot of fun! For Nick and Drew, who first performed together in a high school production of *The Wiz*, it's always a trip sharing their 98° experiences. "Most brothers at this age might be living in different cities and see each other only on the holidays. It's great because we're there for each other. It's an 'I got your back' type of thing," Nick has described.

Nick and Drew don't really fight, though an occasional squabble may crop up. Of course, it's normal for nonrelated bandmates to get annoyed with each other, so imagine two family members being with each other round the clock. But the great thing is that they can be completely honest with each other at all times. "He can say things to me and I won't take it personally," Drew has commented. And as for sibling rivalry, that went out the window a long time ago!

To celebrate their brotherhood, both Nick and Drew got matching armband tattoos with an "L" representing their last name. "We were going to get a family crest," Nick explained, but the two brothers finally settled on their initial.

In fact, there's yet another family member involved in 98°. The guys' mom, Cate, runs the official 98° fan club. She's the one who keeps the fan mail flowing and sends out all their awesome merchandise.

Ultimately, what's really special is that working together means they have the same memories. "Nick's my best friend," Drew told *Popstar!* "He's probably gonna be the best man at my wedding. We can tell each other anything. I can be the one to tell him he's got something stuck in his teeth." Hey, what are brothers for?

We Are Family

"Our grandma worried about everything, especially when Drew first joined the group. I think she feels a little more comfortable knowing we're together and we can look out for each other." — Nick, to *Teen People*

Random Fact

When Nick, the only band member to have a speaking part on *City Guys*, made his acting debut, Drew gave his big bro some pointers. The most important: Be yourself. Duh — he was playing himself.

Things That Make You Say "Awwww"

"He's a great singer and a great performer, so just the chance to work with him on that level is good." — Nick on Drew

Chapter Eight
Love-o-Scopes

How do you know which 98° guy is your best match? It's all in the stars!

Jeff: Taurus
April 30

Taureans are usually known for being really stubborn, but that's not always the case. Determined is a better way to describe them, especially when you're describing Jeff. He's one of the most determined people you'll ever meet. Hey, if it wasn't for Jeff's tenacity, there'd be no 98°! He was the one who stuck with it, throughout all the revolving members in the early '90s.

Taureans are also known for being extremely considerate and thoughtful. That's Jeff all right, he's one of the nicest guys around.

Most Taureans have a great sense of humor. Jeff is a total prankster, always playing a funny on Drew, Justin, or Nick. And he loves to laugh, watch comedy films, and goof off. If you're into being silly, you and Jeff would be well-suited.

Dependable and hilarious Jeff could sweep any girl off her feet. What qualities would a girl have to possess to lift him off his toes? "She can hang out and be one of the guys," he told *Teen Celebrity*. "You can play pool with her, she's your best friend. And she doesn't have to be physically amazing. She'll be beautiful because of that — there's beauty in every single girl alive."

Drew: Leo
August 8

Leos like Drew are known for their love of being in control. That doesn't mean that they need to be right all the time, but they like to keep things as orderly as possible. As Jeff has said, "Drew is the one who's got this group in check." So, if you're disorganized, you'd have to get your act together to get along with Drew.

Leos are also born performers. It's not surprising that Drew ended up on stage! It's his nature, after all. They're definitely not shy — they speak their minds at all times. If you're someone who can handle utter honesty, then you and Drew might be a perfect match. The great thing about Leos is that they're extremely loyal and caring. If Drew was your boyfriend, you can be sure that he'd keep his focus on you.

What does Drew say about his perfect girl? "She must like having a good time. I love fun. I also like a girl who has opinions about things." His biggest criteria for a potential date? Someone who's not conceited. You've got to be down-to-earth, just like Drew!

Who's the most romantic of the band? Check out their Love-o-scopes.

Justin: Pisces
February 25

Justin is the epitome of a Pisces — compassionate and poetic. The fact that he's an artist completely fits the image of a Pisces guy. But the thing about Pisceans is that because of their sensitive souls, they're capable of being hurt very easily. Justin's gone through his share of heartbreak, but that's made him more conscious of bruising other people's feelings. He's definitely the 98° member most likely to keep the peace. Jeff has commented on Justin, "He's very concerned about everybody's well-being. He wants everything to go smoothly." If you like a shy and sweet guy, Justin's right for you!

This Pisces dreamer always has a new idea or a party plan. He's the one who'll go out clubbing whenever he gets some free time. If you're into having a night on the town, you'd have a blast with Justin.

Here's what Justin's said about the girl who'd rock his world: "I like a girl who can be deep and serious, but not deep and serious all the time — and knows how to have fun." Does he sound like your style?

Nick: Scorpio
November 9

If you're looking for a calm, unemotional guy, then Nick is definitely not your type! He's fiery and full of passion about everything from his fave football team to a great new movie he's seen. Nick has strong feelings on just about every subject! That means that you and Nick would have plenty of stuff to talk about. And, like any Scorpio, Nick will tell someone exactly what he thinks of them. Not that he's brutal — he's just really honest.

Scorpios are known for being extremely focused. That's the case with Nick, who never deterred from his dream of making it in showbiz, even when he was working all kinds of jobs just to make ends meet. They're also very hardworking — especially in a relationship. Scorpio dudes enjoy having one girlfriend more than dating around, so you can be sure that if you two clicked, he'd be a great mate.

Nick jokes that "I like girls who like me." But, really, he likes girls who are headstrong. "I like to deal with a little adversity and have a struggle now and then," he's said. If you don't mind a little bit of a roller-coaster relationship, then you and Nick are suited to get to know one another.

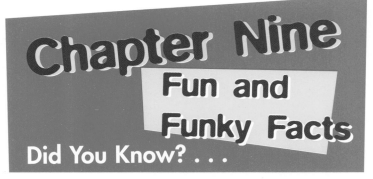

Chapter Nine
Fun and Funky Facts
Did You Know?...

★ Nick's favorite song to perform live is "Invisible Man" because "so many people around the world know the song and sing along." Jeff's is "Because of You" because it's got "a good groove and cool choreography."

★ When the guys first got together they shared a two-bedroom apartment in L.A. and when they moved to New York, they got a four-bedroom place. Talk about togetherness!

★ Nick and Jeff consider themselves the worst dancers of the group!

★ Along with "boy bands" like Backstreet Boys and 'N Sync, MTV named 98° the number two newsmaker in 1998. Who were some of the other top tenners? The Fugees, the Spice Girls, and the Beastie Boys.

★ In Jeff's football days, he was 40 pounds heavier. Yikes!

★ The first song 98° ever completely produced and wrote themselves was, fittingly, "Completely," from their debut album.

★ Even though he's used to being recognized as a celebrity, Nick doesn't want people to treat him like a star. "They think you deserve special privileges, they kind of place you on a pedestal."

★ Justin's most-prized possession is his CD collection.

★ The guys were into singing a cappella in their early days because they couldn't afford instruments.

★ Jeff's afraid of heights. He had to try hard to remain calm when they filmed high up at the top of San Francisco's Golden Gate Bridge for the "Because of You" video.

★ These major sports fans have performed the national anthem at several athletic events, but their first time was singing at an L.A. Dodgers/Cincinnati Reds game.

★ It's no secret that Boyz II Men are 98°'s all-time idols. They finally got to meet them last year.

When you're 98° and your popularity's rising, there's not much time to chill!

★ *98° and Rising* is the first album in which Justin and Drew got to sing lead. They both get some solo time on "Do You Want to Dance?" and Drew shines on "Still."

★ 98° have received some odd gifts in their travels, including pet turtles in Malaysia and a 12-pound bar of Toblerone chocolate that Nick lugged back from Switzerland.

How to Reach Them:
On the Web — Their official site is www.98degrees.com
Their Fan Club — You can write them at:
98° Worldwide Fan Club
PO Box 31379
Cincinnati, OH 45231
USA

Nick and Jeff pal around at the Motown Cafe in New York.

It's never too hot for cool leather jackets—even if you're 98°!

What's up next? Jeff, Justin, Nick, and Drew contemplate an amazing future.

Chapter Ten
Futurama

With the success of *98° and Rising*, Nick, Drew, Justin, and Jeff are excited to stay on the road and bring more of their music to fans everywhere. They have absolutely no plans of slowing down. The guys will continue touring all summer long, taking their funky blend of pop and R&B to another level. After all, 98°'s biggest priority is having their fans appreciate their music. "There's no better feeling than people actually loving what you do," says Nick. And along with all that great music are plans to make the world a better place with the 98° Foundation. Adds Justin, "We want to make a difference."